Mrs. Burta

Alamo Across Texas

JILL STOVER

Alamo

For Anna and Clare, sister travelers

First Edition 1 2 3 4 5 6 7 8 9 10

Library of Congress Cataloging in Publication Data
Stover, Jill. Alamo across Texas / by Jill Stover.
      p.   cm. Summary: When a drought dries up his perfect river home, Alamo the alligator sets off
to find a new place to live. ISBN 0-688-11712-0. — ISBN 0-688-11713-9 (lib. bdg.) [1. Alligators—
Fiction. 2. Texas—Fiction.] I. Title. PZ7.S8887A1 1992 [E]—dc20 91-47572 CIP AC

Across Texas

Lothrop, Lee & Shepard Books   New York

On the Lavaca River in the great state of
Texas, there once lived an alligator named Alamo.
Life along the river suited Alamo perfectly.

He had plenty of water, lots of tasty fishes, a
fine shade tree, and an interesting assortment
of friends and neighbors.

But one year there came a drought. Day after day
the sun beat down,

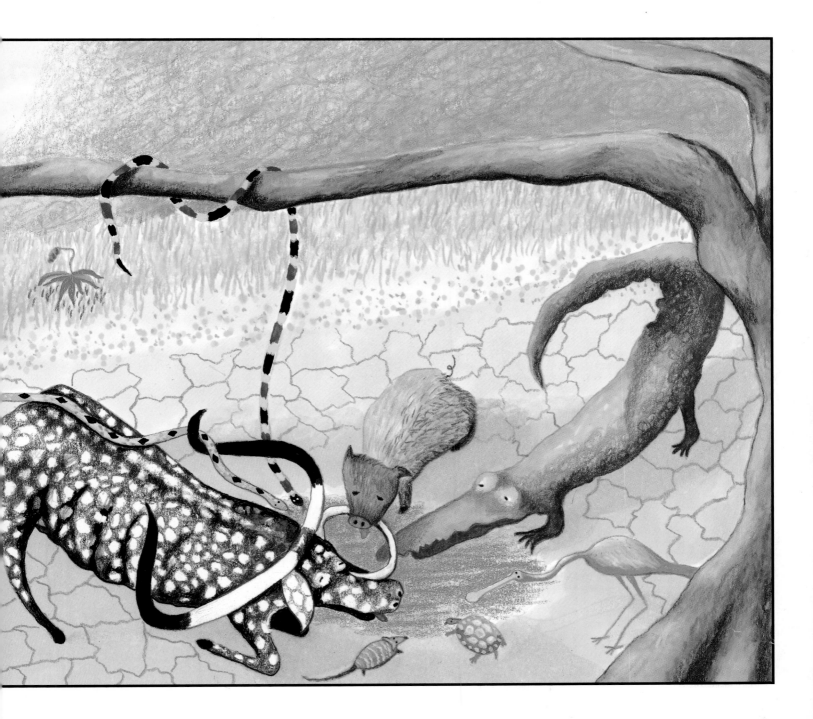

until there was no more water, no more tasty
fishes, no more shade tree . . .

and no more friends and neighbors.

Life along the river was no longer pleasant at all. So Alamo set off down the trail to find a new home.

He walked and he walked

and he walked and he walked . . .

until he came to a Texas ranch.

The ranch had water . . .

but no tasty fishes, and his new neighbors were
too curious. So Alamo hit the trail again.

He walked and he walked and he walked and he walked, until he came to the ocean. There were lots of tasty fishes . . .

but the water was rough and far too salty. So
Alamo hit the trail again.

He walked and he walked and he walked and he walked, until he came to a swimming pool. The pool was full of water . . .

but there were no tasty fishes, and it was far
too crowded. So Alamo hit the trail again.

He walked and he walked and he walked
and he walked . . .

until he came to a city.

The city had water *and* fishes . . .

but what a racket! It didn't smell too good either.
So Alamo hit the trail again.